Best Wishes!

Anthony Valerio

2017

# Praise for *Dante in Love*

"A unique and marvelous window onto a classical masterpiece!

"There are many ways of "translating" a work of literature. Valerio translates this noble work of medieval courtly love into a new medium, one that is vibrant, compelling, and immediately accessible to the broadest spectrum of today's readers. He tells and comments at the same time, in language that is insightful and compassionate. Dante's story becomes the story of a young "anyman" in love, a passion that comes down to us through the ages cloaked in different shades yet comprised of the same anxieties, hopes and dreams. The telling is encased in a degree of comic irony that makes the voice and the story all the more enjoyable".—Gonzo 50

"I love all the drama. So many favorite moments. 'Beatrice joins a gaggle of ladies to mock Dante' was my number one rated drama. A dopey, voyeur Dante-guy goes to funerals where women are grieving and spies and grabs the attention. Valerio keeps the drama in the foreground. But he doesn't intrude too much in the narrative. It's still the Dante-guy's story.

Valerio does much more than 'translate' that story, and there's such good balance to the conjoined voices. Love and sex are both startling, funny, serious, culture-bound, crazy, and kind of entrepreneurial..."

I like how the book shines a light on 'moving on' in terms of the writing process. How do you move beyond writing obsessions that drag you in and maybe down? Valerio and Dante do some judicious workshopping for all the struggling writers.

Valerio's modern writer's voice comes out in the translation. I can kind of see his face as he looks at a man on his knees with horror and empathy. I love Valerio's vocabulary: love how Mr. Love 'bullied' the weak-kneed lover. There is comedy in the Anthony-language, and that makes me think it could have been in

Dante-writer too."

What I like: Valerio takes the religious, church father Medieval out of the Dante in his own way. He leaves us the medieval 'mystery of love'."

—Keala J. Jewel, Professor of Italian Language and Literature, Emerita. Dartmouth College

*DANTE IN LOVE*

Dante Alighieri's *Vita Nuova Reinterpreted*

### *Also by Anthony Valerio*

*The Mediterranean Runs Through Brooklyn.* Italian edition, *Brooklyn Mediterraneo (Zona)*

*Valentino and the Great Italians*

*BART: a Life of A. Bartlett Giamatti*

*Conversation with Johnny, a novel*

*Anita Garibaldi, a Biography.* Italian edition, *Anita (Gallucci)*

*The Little Sailor, a Romantic Thriller*

*Toni Cade Bambara's One Sicilian Night*

*John Dante's Inferno, a Playboy's Life*

*Immigrants according to Anthony Valerio - volume I (e-edition)*

*Immigrants according to Anthony Valerio - volume II (e-edition)*

*Immigrants according to Anthony Valerio - volumes I & II first edition(paperback)*

**ANTHONY VALERIO**

*DANTE IN LOVE*

Cover drawing of Beatrice by ©Tony Palladino http://www.tonypalladino.com. By permission of his estate.

Author's note: interactive answers can be sent to anthony@anthonyvalerio.com for consideration in the *Dante in Love* blog.

ISBN: 978-0-9904675-6-4

Library of Congress Control Number: 2017911901

All inquiries please contact

anthony@anthonyvalerio.com

*for* *Ellen V. Nerenberg*

## Introduction

Dante Alighieri (1265-1321), author of the monumental work *The Divine Comedy*, properly titled *The Comedy*, wrote his little book of about fifty pages entitled *Vita nova* [i] around the age of twenty-seven, early in his career. Supposedly, it's the real story of Dante and Beatrice, of a tormented lover and writer of prose and poetry and an elusive young woman named Beatrice. Some say that very little happens in their story: they meet at the age of nine; he falls for her hard; for reasons known only to him, he tries to hide his affection, seducing and using other women as shields and fails; Beatrice dies; and Dante spends the rest of the work lamenting and praising her. But much more *happens*.

Dante's readers are put through their paces in an attempt to grasp the story, in modern parlance get our heads around it, as it is shrouded in ambiguity and allure. He does not mention his name nor the name of his city nor even the name of the major river that flows through it. His work is at once generic and particular. We, his readers, know the names and places of these gaps. We contribute to the great work's grandeur with our own intelligence and imagination.

I have tried to show how Dante achieved his wondrous effects and the literary devices he employed, drawing on my experience as a writer and book editor.


He's Dante. His city is Florence. His river is the Arno. He's also the--

Lover.


And Beatrice, who was she? Human, an idea, dawn, God? One woman? An assemblage of many? Yes, she was his bliss, his happiness, his joy and his muse. He provides her given name, mentioning "Beatrice" once. Leaving out his own name and their town and their river illuminate her all the more. Names, then, were the consequence of things. Beauty, Beatitude, Bliss, Beatific—she was all these things. Therefore, she's Beatrice.

She's also the -

Beloved.

I wanted to penetrate and understand the nature of the poet's undying, unrequited love for her, as it proved forceful and persisted throughout my decades as a practitioner and, yes, also as a Lover and Beloved. I felt that in *Vita nova* there was a grand love story but one always slightly out of reach. At the same time, my heart, and perhaps others', soared and sank along with the tormented lover's. It's like I, we, insist on making our way through the nebula shrouding this great work of centuries past. The story and its ideas, feelings and curiosities followed me and have proved immensely enticing, worthy of the attempt to achieve some consummation in a re-telling, a quest to caress.

And who does not like a good love story?

For the sake of that good beguiling story to emerge and crystallize, I have compressed and modernized Dante's words in Italian into English, from the point of view of my life as a writer. I have found translations of *A New Life* wanting, not so much in their competency as in attempts to bring the original text to narrative life in an exciting way. Dante says he wrote *Vita nova* in the vernacular, the vulgar Latin tongue, which is a version of the Italian language spoken today, so that women could understand it. Texts normally were written in Latin at the time and for learned readers. Not only have I tried to uncover and elucidate the story that is there to be read, but also recover the one to be spoken by the same women to whom he addressed it.

This modern interpretation, I hope, will make the great artist's work accessible to younger generations, old faithfulls as well. For example, translations have used numbered sections, breaking the rhythm, while Dante wrote the original unnumbered, letting his prose and poems flow like the clear Arno flowing through Florence. I have sought to bring this modern text close to readers of Dante by making it interactive, almost as if it were the secret diary of a young man's outpouring of his or her broken heart to be shared by young and old, prompting responses if so desired.

I found more than one story, a story within a story. Yes, a young man's unfulfilled powerful love for a young woman out of reach but also another story almost in code: the story of a writer in formation, one experimenting with prose and poetry in the same work, employing the Beloved as blood and bone but also as disembodied muse, idea, nature, god—all of which contribute to an eternal love.

I have taken liberties, reducing redundancies and explanations of poetry parts for the sake of keeping the story moving, at the same time reverential and always faithful to the original text. I have not translated word for word. I have culled the story from the Italian vernacular as he wrote it to an English vernacular. The original will always, always be there.

AV 2017

Their little book was saved in his memory and in that part before which little could be read a chapter[ii] heading appeared: *Incipit vita nova,* Here begins a new life. His plan was to transcribe the words beneath that heading into this new book, if not all those words at least their gist.

Nine times since his birth the heaven of light [iii], or the sun, had almost returned to the same point, and the heaven of fixed stars had moved one twelfth of a degree [iv] to the east when *la gloriosa donna de la mia mente,*[v] the glorious lady of his mind, appeared before his eyes for the first time. Imagine loving someone so much that you measure their birth by the sun and the stars.

I measure my love for_____by

_____.

Many who had no idea what to call her,

called her Beatrice. She was precisely eight years four months of age and Dante was nine. It's said that Dante was born in May and she in June. Lilies splashed golden like the heaven of light, and women and men in Florence and around the world convened to celebrate workers and their work for it was the feast day of *Calindimaggio,* May Day, which fell on the first day of the month of flowers in their time as it does in ours.

The feast day was held at the house of Folco Portinari, a prominent Florentine hosting this feast day because the Church of St. Michael's was in disrepair. Who but a great powerful man could stand in for the parish church? The good prior Folco invited families high and low, like Bellincione di Alighiero, said to be a money lender and minor landowner, and his son Dante. Boys and girls skipped around the decorative May Pole, holding onto streamers of every color of the rainbow which were attached on top to a common wheel which turned round 'n round. Little Dante took hold of a streamer and skipped, then, his head spinning, he found himself in the estate's grand vestibule in the shadows of a cluster of festive men. Suddenly,

Beatrice appeared up on the landing and began descending the wide, sweeping staircase. He may have been nine years old but it's not the boy who described her now. Her dress [vi]was of a most noble color, crimson, girded and adorned in a style suitable for a nine-year-old girl, with humility and purity. The vital spirit of his most secret chamber, that part of us that no one else knows--this precious, private substance began to tremble so violently, like a metronome gone awry, that faraway vessels of his body--his toes, the follicles of hair on his head-- shook terribly, and this vibrating vital spirit [vii]said in Latin:

*Ecce deus fortior me, qui veniens dominabitur michi.* Here's a god stronger than I who has come to rule.

These powerful words, echoing, traveled to the animal spirit, the one in the high chamber to which like busy termites all the senses bring their perceptions. The animal spirit was amazed, prompting it to speak directly to the spirit of sight:

*"Apparuit iam beatitudo vestra."* "Your bliss has arrived."

The boy was --

Lovestruck.

He wasn't going to eat or sleep or talk. The spirit of his stomach growled:

*"Heu miser, quia frequenter impeditus ero deinceps!"* "You're gonna be jammed up like this, pal."

The first time my love and I met was_____

_____.

The spirits of the Lover's imagination and memory and at the same time his longing for the Beloved resurrected her image as it appeared when he first beheld her, in a crimson dress suitable to her age, descending her father's staircase. This image was in front of him all the time--in thin air; when he closed his eyes there she was, in a blood-red dress set against the infinite blackness. In this way Amor, Love, was born. From that time on, Love lorded over his soul which readily became Love's betrothed. Love grew so assured and tyrannical through the power the boy's imagination lent to him that he, young Dante, couldn't help but obey Amor's every wish.

"Go and seek out this *angiola giovanissima*," Amor commanded him many times when he was a boy. The Lover went in search of his young angel in places which he doesn't designate so that we can imagine where he might have beheld her. Across the road from Folco's estate on dark, rainy days. Amid high winds tossing the arbors that had stood so tall and still that first spring day. Perhaps she stood in her room in the glow of candlelight. He mingled in the crowd taking the early evening community stroll, an eye out for her. He watched her from the last pew in their small parish chapel, the large Folco family occupying the first one, closer to the tabernacle and to God. And he saw her to be of such noble and laudable behavior that to describe her now Dante drew on Homer's *Iliad* [viii], using words uttered by King Priam of Ilium over the corpse of the great warrior Hector, his best son and favorite of the gods for burning the thigh bones of heifers and unblemished goats. Dante substituted the feminine pronoun "she".

*Ella non parea figliuola d'uomo mortale, ma di deo.* She did not seem the daughter of ordinary men, but of a God.

Though the image of the Beloved dressed in noble crimson descending her father's staircase was constantly before him--one of Love's tricks to dominate him--it was so potent that it never allowed Amor to take over without the trusted advice of Reason, at least for a while.

Panacea for Lovesickness--

LOVE accompanied by REASON.

When I feel lovesick, I_____.

Many days had passed till they added up to exactly nine years since the first appearance of this *gentilissima.* On the last of these days she appeared again dressed in the purest white, flanked by two older women. It was precisely the ninth hour, that is, three o'clock in the afternoon. As she walked down a street she turned her eyes toward where he was standing with great apprehension and greeted him[ix] "with ineffable graciousness which today is rewarded in the eternal life." So Beatrice had died *before* he transcribed the crux of the words of their little memory book, and she'll die again in the real time of this story. Beatrice is dead and she's alive, a device used also by today's fiction writers especially when memory is involved. The few words of her angelic voice delighted him. He left his companions and returned as if intoxicated to the loneliness of his room, where he set about thinking of *questa cortesissima.* He collapsed onto his thin mattress of hay and fell into a gentle slumber in which a marvelous vision [x] arose of a cloud the color of fire in his room and inside this cloud he made out the figure of a man--Signor Amor! who was fearsome yet wonderful to behold. He spoke forcefully—

*"Ego dominus tuus."* "I'm your master."

A sleeping, naked woman wrapped loosely in a crimson cloth lay in Love's arms. The Dreamer's Eye approached the woman, closer, closer—hey, it was the Lady of the Virtuous Greeting! One of Amor's hands held an object all ablaze. Said Amor:

*"Vide cor tuum."* "Behold your heart."

Outside it was between nine and ten o'clock,

first of the last nine hours of night, and the starry heavens shone down on Florence and on his sleeping form and on his vision.

Then Signor Amor woke up the naked, loosely-clad woman and with the persuasive power of his art made her eat the burning object in his hand, his heart, which she did, hesitantly. After a while, inexplicably, Love's happiness turned to bitter weeping. He gathered her in his arms and they rose toward the heavens, causing the dreamer such anguish, twisting and turning on his crinkled straw, that he bolted awake.

Dante's method in *The New Life*[xi] was to conjoin prose and poetry, usually prose first then poetry in the form of sonnets [xii], ballads [xiii] and songs. It's said that in *Vita Nova,* Dante had first written the poems and then wrapped prose accounts around them in order to make a cohesive book. The poetic form of the prose [xiv]offers more detail and insight and in general elevates the work as a whole. At this point he composed a sonnet addressed *A ciascun'alma presa e gentil core.* To every loving heart and captive soul. Dante was in the habit of addressing his poems to specific audiences, especially those who understood and were capable of returning the love contained in the poems themselves. The poetic form of the prose continues:

*It was toward nine o'clock in the evening, every star shining, when Amor appeared.*

*I tremble at the memory.*

*Love seemed merry as he held my heart in his hand and, in his arms, he held*

*my lady, asleep, wrapped in a cloth.*

*Then he woke her up and, afraid, she ate my burning heart.*

*Afterward, I saw Love depart, weeping.*

Only recently discovering his abilities as a poet, and ambitious, Dante was determined to make his sonnet known to the famous poets of the time.[xv] He asked them to interpret his vision, kind of like appealing to a panel of illustrious poet-therapists for their reactions. Poet Guido Cavalcanti[xvi] (1255-1300) responded with a sonnet of his own[xvii], which begins: *Vedeste, al mio parere, onne valore...* In my opinion you saw all that's worthy... As a result, Cavalcanti became first among his friends.

But no one got the true interpretation of his dream, Dante claimed. There was only one true interpretation and only he, its bearer, knew it. "But now," he wrote further--*now* perhaps meaning once their little book had been transcribed and read by most of the women in Florence--"its meaning was very clear, even to the least sophisticated."

My interpretation of Dante's dream: _____

_____.

His vision reduced him to a total physical mess because his soul was obsessed with thoughts of his *gentilissima*. He barely ate or slept, grew pale, weak, frail and in public stuck out like a sore thumb. His friends worried about him. Others, recognizing Signor Amor's punishing work, and therefore envious—there were a few sadomasochists in Florence—wanted to know what he wished to keep secret from everybody else. It had to be because of a woman—but who? Was she able to read the vulgar tongue? Married? Had they fornicated? He had to respond in order to stem the rising tide of these *malelingue*. Seeing that they could easily read

Amor's signs on his face, he decided on a generic response of some verisimilitude:

Amore...m'avea governato. Love...had governed me, he offered by the will of Love, who was still directing him according to Reason's counsel.

But his explanation provoked more prurient interest. "Love, yeah, but who for?"

He stared deeply into their inquisitive eyes but then an eerie smile, slow and cautious, broke across his drawn face and, with his eyes shining like stars, he said nothing.

One Sunday the Beloved was sitting in a place where words about the Queen of Glory, the Virgin Mary, were being heard; that is, in their small, cozy chapel. My lady and I have visited their chapel all these centuries later. Silence and stillness pervade, and it is dark, and pilgrims such as ourselves can sense their ancient presence. The Beloved sat in one of the first pews and the Lover in the rear. His eyes fixed on her narrow back and shoulders, the nape of her neck, her veiled head. No matter how hard he tried to avert his eyes, they kept returning to her, so for reasons known only to his deepest regions, his obsessive compulsion for Beatrice had to be camouflaged.

I think he had to hide his feelings for her because_____.

He needed a go-between, someone, something between himself and Beatrice. A lady of very pleasing aspect sat at the center of a straight line beginning at Beatrice and ending in his eyes. This Screen Lady, sensing a pair of eyes blazing into her back, turned around and, amazed, saw a young man in a rear pew with a consumptive face and hollowed-out eyes staring straight at her. Quickly she did an about-face to the altar, then, after the Mass moved forward, turned around again—he was still staring! The rustling of her silk garments drowned out the monsignor's words about the Queen of Glory, causing parishioners to look around at the source of the noise, the Screen Lady, then all eyes followed hers further back to their object, Dante. On leaving the chapel he overheard:

*"Vedi come cotale donna distrugge la*

*persona di costui."* "See how that woman has destroyed that one over there--nodding in his direction."

They named the Screen Lady and in this way he realized that these discerning, easily-led parishioners were referring to the lady who'd been in direct line between the Beloved and his adoring eyes. He felt tremendous relief, assured at least on this day that the true object of his gaze hadn't been revealed. But wait—if he could fool parishioners at Sunday mass, maybe he could fool everybody all the days of the year. And that's what he did. He made this poor woman a permanent shield of the truth. His true love of one woman didn't prevent him from loving another falsely, from making her the sacrificial lamb. For months then years he played the part of false lover. Did he bring her bouquets of lilies of the field? Sit beside her in chapel? Take the evening stroll alongside her, hand-in-hand? For what better way to camouflage his true feelings for one woman than to appear with another in the same places. Make love to her convincingly, evincing from her eyes that cosmic glow of supreme corporeal satisfaction so that everyone could see and therefore know all the more erroneously? Before long, most of the people who talked about him thought they knew his secret. You can't possibly adore a woman like this over a period of years completely disingenuously. To bolster people's errant belief even more as well as the tragic Screen Lady's that he truly loved her, he dedicated certain little poems to her. But these aren't included in the little book of his memory except to the extent that they spoke of Beatrice. He decided to omit them all. Maybe down the road he'd mention those in praise of her.

As a way of momentarily visiting the truth, the desire rose in the Lover to write down the Beloved's name. If he couldn't demonstrate his love for her to the world, at least he could inscribe her name and look at it and repeat it—"Beatrice! Beatrice! Beatrice!" like a mantra, in this roundabout way have her materialize and pervade only *his* entire being. But he couldn't set down her name alone, for no woman or man is a recorded island. How to write it down and at the same time keep it secret? He could have kept the piece of paper in his pocket or in a drawer forever, but writing for Dante had wings. Well, he could surround her name with the names of other ladies, especially the gentlewoman's with which his name was romantically linked. Then *her* name and indirectly *herself* would attract the most attention, and the world would believe this was just another way for the poet to demonstrate his love for her. The other names would simply be window dressing. So he wrote down the names of 60 of the most beautiful women which the Almighty had placed in their city. To know the names of 60 beautiful living women in his city or any city then as much as now, you had to have had an eye out for feminine beauty for some time. Ogle? Fantasize over? Keep up with the gossip? That was our Poet/Lover. He wrote down the 60 names in the form of a *serventese* [xviii], a satiric poem, placing Beatrice's name even further from direct attachment. But he didn't include his satire in their little book nor would he have mentioned it had not her name appeared miraculously as the ninth among the 60 names. That is, he wrote down 60 names in no pre-determined order, the sole guideline being that each name call up a beautiful woman of Florence. Whichever name came to mind first he'd write that one then the next and so on. It would've been interesting to know which women's names preceded and, inspired by her name, followed "Beatrice." Point is, miraculously, "Beatrice" refused to appear beside any other number save nine.

Providing the Screen Lady with a brief reprieve from the disgrace unknown to her, she was called away to a distant town, hurling the deceitful poet topsy-turvy. His cover was suddenly blown! What would he do left alone? He felt awful, more so than he would've believed possible. Had Signor Amor turned the tables, instilling him with true feelings of love for the Screen Lady?

But Dante continued his wily ways, deciding that if he failed to make a show of grief over her departure at least a little, people might believe he'd loved another all along, so he scribbled a few words of unhappiness which their little book includes because many of those words were intended for Beatrice.

O you who travel [xix]along Love's path, stop

and look around for anyone whose grief surpasses mine, and I beg only that you hear me out then judge whether I'm not the keeper and place of every torment. Not for any worth found in me but through his own nobility, Love provided me with the serenity and sweetness of the Lover's life, to the extent that I often overheard: "Wow! Is he lucky! God, what qualities of heart does he possess to warrant such joy?" Now all's spent of love's treasure trove--look how impoverished I've become! Like those who conceal their want for shame, I display a merry exterior but in my heart struggo e pluro, I melt into tears.

Once his problematic girlfriend was out of town, the Poet may have been looking for something to write about and found two powerful sonnets: one focusing on Love and the other on Death. It was easy, almost natural, for him to find a circuitous, back-channel way of including them: a young virtuous, much admired, woman dies whom he'd seen in Beatrice's company. The custom was for men to grieve outside the deceased's house while women grieved inside--grieving being gender sensitive, co-grieving sullying pure sorrow. Or perhaps men seeing women up close in moments of extreme grief, like wailing or pulling out of the hair or rocking back and forth imploring the Heavens was overbearing. Dante was among the group of men outside the house, peering in. *Holy smokes I know her!* How could he forget? He'd seen the deceased several times in the Beloved's company so he was unable to hold back his tears.

Majestic Mr. Love in human form was inside grieving with the women, looming over the charming young woman's body. Often he raised his head heavenward where *l'alma gentil* already dwelled, she who'd been of such gentle aspect.

**Love:**

"Weep, Lovers, for Love weeps as you hear why he cries. Love listens, he hears women crying Pity, showing bitter grief in their eyes 'cause villainous death has snatched a gentle heart, spoiling that which is most praiseworthy in the world, *sovra de l'onore*, above honor."

We glimpse a value Dante held high, one that superseded all others in a gentlewoman--modesty.

**Death** is--

Cruel, Pity's enemy, *di dolor madre antica,* ancient mother of grief. Dante gets personal: his tongue tires from bawling Death out. He's capable of dominating Death by making him beg for mercy "by stating your crime, your guilt for every wrong, by unveiling it to all people, by arousing anger in those who will love."

Then Dante indicts Death directly:

"You've severed courtesy and the virtuous found in praising women. *...in gaia gioventute distrutta hai l'amorosa leggiadria.* ...in gay youth you've destroyed love's lightheartedness."

Then something happened which made him leave Florence and go toward, but not exactly reach, the place where the Screen Lady was staying. Away on business? Off to war? The journey bothered him because it took him farther and farther away from his joy. His sighs couldn't soothe his heart's anguish.

Riding along, he came upon Amor in the middle of the road in the shape of a pilgrim wearing thin, threadbare clothes, forlorn, his eyes trained on the ground except when he lifted and turned his head toward the beautiful, crystal-clear Arno that flowed alongside. Amor called out to him:

"I come from the lady who's been your defense for a long time. She won't be coming back to your city any time soon. That heart which I made you leave with her, I have with me now and am taking it to a lady who will be your new defense."

Amor the Matchmaker!

Once again his heart was on the move. Amor had given it to Beatrice, had taken it and held it aflame in the dream wherein the Beloved ate it. Now he took it from one Screen Lady and gave it to another.

Along the Road of Sighs, Amor named this Screen Lady #2, which Dante recognized immediately. He doesn't reveal her name or anything about her. He keeps us guessing, imagining. Then Amor, forever wily, cautioned:

"If you have to repeat any of what I've told

you, do it in such a way that people can't figure out the fake love you've shown which you will continue to show but to this other lady."

Dante merged so completely with Mr. Love that the latter vanished, the poet didn't know how. And then all that day he rode along the narrow path beside the splendid stream, pensive, sighing.

Once back home the Lover searched out Screen Lady #2 and, using Amor's unfailing GPS, found her. To make a long story short, Dante writes—the long story being he pretended to love her for months and years; how must he have felt?; did his Screen Women ever entertain any doubts? He seduced this second victim by way of his singular purpose of establishing new camouflage of the truth. In a short time, he fashioned the poor woman so completely into a go-between that many people commented beyond the bounds of courtesy. Such public displays of affection—kissing! caressing! god only knows what they did behind the boudoir door! The question was: Would these scurrilous speculations find their way to his most gentle lady? Which is exactly what happened. Because of the outcry that was making him out to be infamous for vice, one day while walking along a certain street Beatrice, destroyer of all vice, queen of virtue, denied him of her greeting.

How instrumental was her marvelous greeting? In anticipation of it, he held no man his enemy. A flame of charity burned inside him which made him forgive all trespasses, like confessing his sins and saying penance and forgiving himself for betrayals, fabrications, outright lies. Now if anyone asked him anything, his sole response, uttered with a face filled with humility, could only have been--

Love.

And when she was about to greet him— slightest turn of her head in his direction, parting of her lips, smile beginning to break—one of Love's spirits drove out sight's feeble ones and said: *"Andate a onorare la donna vostra,"* "Go honor your lady" then took its place. Do you want to know about love? Just look at his trembling eyes. And when, finally, her greeting found him--her words: their sound/timbre/echo—Love was no longer the means to veil his intolerable bliss. Rather, possessed by an excess of sweetness, Love became such that the Lover's body, completely under Amor's rule, often moved like a heavy inanimate object.

Imagine his state when she held back her "Hey there!"

I'm a mess when my love_____.

He withdrew from all company and found a solitary place in which to cry--an alley, shadowy corner under a bridge--where he bathed the earth in bitter tears. Once he got hold of himself, reduced to gasps so that on his way home he wouldn't be a public spectacle, he closed himself in his room where he could carry on with nobody listening. "Holy Mother, pity me!" he called and, in the same breadth, beseeched Love himself: "Hey Love, help me!"

He fell asleep, crying "...like a little boy who'd just been spanked." Halfway through his slumber he thought he saw a young man in his room dressed in sheer white garments, looking worried. The phantasm stared down and said, sighing--

"*Fili mi, tempus est ut pretermictantur*

*simulacra nostra."* "My son, it's time to put aside our pretences."

All of the Poet/Lover' deceptions—false affection, double-meaning sonnets and songs—hadn't fooled Beatrice one iota. She'd been on to him, thus refusing to greet him.

But if she'd seen the adverse effects her salutation had on him and deprived him of it, she was, nevertheless, as her name signifies supremely benevolent. In any case, it was time for a change.

He seemed to know the young man in white clothes, he'd called out to him the same way in dreams past. Dante's Dream Repertory of Players. Yes—it was Love himself! And he was weeping from compassion and, at the same time, anxious that Dante say something.

The Dreamer complied: "Lord of all virtues, why are you crying?"

Shifting sharply from feelings of sorrow and anxiety to that of cool self-assessment, Amor responded:

"I'm like the center of a circle equidistant

from all points in the circumference, but you're not."

What a nugget of wisdom! Lovers, conduct yourselves in a centered way![xx] Dante was self-helping through Dream Work.

So long had young Dante been in denial of his slippery ways, perhaps believing that deception in service of divine love was a form of love, and so profound was his need to cloak his true feelings, he didn't understand Amor's words.

"Say what, my Lord?"

Love responded in the vernacular so all those women could comprehend:

*"Non dimandare più che utile ti sia."*
"Don't ask more than's useful to you."[xxi]

Without rhyme or reason the dreamer shifted discourse to Beatrice's refusal to give him the time of day. Dante, ever passionate:

"Why, O Lord?"

Amor answered directly:

"Our Beatrice heard from certain big mouths that you were harming the lady I'd named on the Road of Sighs"—Screen Lady #2—"and feared you're also a source of harm even to her."

Agent of harm to one woman, same to another. Though an isolated creation, the Beloved was the only one who knew the fabricator's penchant for harming others. Love continued:

"Since your cover has been blown, at least with Screen Lady #2, I want you to write a poem in which you mention the powers that I, Love, have over you and that every since you were a boy of nine you've belonged to her, your only joy. Call as witness he who knows misery--myself! and beg him to   testify on your behalf. He'll gladly explain it to her. As a result, she'll understand your true feelings and also the back story of the evil tongues. Let these words be an intermediary, don't speak directly to her—I'll say them. And don't send these words to any place where she could hear them except in my company. Enhance your words with sweet music."

Then Love disappeared and Dante awoke. In his lonely room he composed a ballad, his words set to sweet music meant to be sung during a dance, in which words and melody and choreography followed exactly what Amor had instructed. It begins:

>*Ballata, i'voi che tu ritrovi Amore...* Ballad[xxii],
> I wish you to seek out Love...

So his effort at an apology was also further removed, beseeching the ballad itself to seek out Love and accompany him into his lady's presence for the purpose of explaining his faults. It wasn't good to go without Love 'cause Beatrice was angry with him and could show disrespect. Along with sweet music, the ballad should first ask for pity then say that Love was right there with them. Love who, as a result of her beauty, turned pale so she should consider well why he'd made him, Dante, look at another woman, remembering his heart has never strayed. Say, ballad, "My lady, his heart has remained steadfast, his entire mind bent on serving you. He's been yours from the start. If she doesn't believe you, tell her to talk to Love." The poor guy was on his knees. "Finally, ballad, beg her, if she can't bring herself to forgive me, to order me by messenger to die and I will obey. And tell Love, compassion's key, to remain with her awhile and say whatever you wish about your servant."

The ballad's penultimate line, asking ballad to tell Love, such concepts understanding one another:

> "...s'ella per tuo prego li perdona, fa che li
> annunzi un bel sembiante pace." "...if
> through your request she forgives him, let
> her kindly face promise peace."

Did he receive some sign that the Beloved had at least heard his ballad, some message, missive of her own? Did he go himself to see with his own eyes whether it had struck a sympathetic ear, inspired a kindly face? But no, not this embattled poet—peace which he so ardently desired was hindered by the assault of four diverse thoughts against which he was defenseless.

1st-- Love's lordship is good for he diverts his faithful from all evil.

Lovers being weak-minded, easily tempted.

2nd--Love's lordship is evil for the more loyalty his faithful give to him, the more grave and pitiful the tribulations he must endure.

This thought had particular purchase with

Dante.

3<sup>rd</sup>--Love's name is so sweet to the ear its sole effect is—sweet!

The way the name Beatrice is the consequence of Beatitude, Love is the consequence of Sweetness.

4<sup>th</sup>--The lady through which Love binds you is unlike other ladies in that her heart can easily be moved.

If Beatrice was of blood and bone, she would've taken offence at this axiom.

These four battling thoughts stymied him like one who doesn't know which road to take. He wants to start out but is stuck. Trying to find a common road where all four thoughts converged was simply not his way; namely, surrendering into pity's arms.

The prose's content finds its way into the poetic form:

> All my thoughts speak of Love;
>
> and display such great diversity
>
> that one makes me desire power,
>
> another says Love's dominion is crazy,

another brings me sweetness through hope,

another brings me frequently to tears;

they agree only over begging for pity, my heart trembling with fear.


Then a good friend maybe recognizing that he needed a change of pace took him to a wedding ritual[xxiii] in which the bride took her first dinner in the new groom's home. The beautiful, happy women on display, around twenty-five of them, would bring Dante pleasure, thought the friend. Women only, much like today's Bridal Shower that occurs prior to matrimony. Women getting together before the men take over. Apparently the sporting friend didn't know about Beatrice's place in his life-- hard to imagine a good friend unaware of this—and unwittingly delivered Dante to the brink of death.

"Why have we come to see these women?" he asked his friend, trusting him.

"To ensure they're served in a worthy manner," replied the friend loftily, revealing himself as much an incurable romantic as Dante, having come not to ogle but to serve the spectacular beauty in attendance.

But serve in what manner? Help carry the wedding dress train? Simply view as some sort of spectacular? Group chaperone? The women could have fun but not by themselves, it seemed.

Most likely they'd changed from formal wedding party attire into comfortable, everyday clothes, freeing them to be more like themselves on this joyful, hopeful occasion—something to see.

Well, ok, I'll please my friend and pay homage to these ladies, Dante decided.

Suddenly, he felt a tremor on the left side of his chest which in no time spread to the rest of his body. Surreptitiously, he rested against the frescoed wall that ran around the house's circumference. Fearing that the others would notice his trembling, he raised his eyes toward the women and saw—o God!--the most gracious Beatrice! She was one of the wedding ensemble! Her sheer presence had emboldened Love who, with his new-found strength so close to her, overwhelmed the spirits of Dante's other senses, tossing some out, killing others, save that of sight. Love wanted eyes for that wondrous lady all his own.

Though in an altered vulnerable state, Dante

felt sorry for the displaced little spirits which, in their turn, lamented:

"If this big fella hadn't bullied us, we'd be able to gaze on the wonder that is Beatrice."

Dante on behalf of the little guy, the kind ordinary women of his day--that is, his ideal readership--knew quite well. Like Americans, who root for the underdog.

The women noticed his transfiguration and cruelly, to his horror, began to mock him and worse, mock him to Beatrice! mimicking some poor pathetic lovesick guy--rolling their eyes, doubling over, swooning. Then perhaps the worst thing happened to him in their little book--Beatrice joined the others in making fun of him!

The friend took Dante by the hand and whisked him away. "What happened to you?" asked this dauntless friend, puzzled.

Dante, his deadened spirits slowly returning to their proper organs--"My feet reached the boundaries of life beyond which one cannot expect to return."

He took leave of his friend and returned to

his Room of Tears where naturally he wept and felt ashamed, saying to himself:

"If she had been aware of my sorry state, if she'd known how Love took over my spirits' senses, making me wretched, she wouldn't have mocked the way I looked. She would've pitied me."

Growing more confident of his poetry than his prose, he confronted her directly in a poem on the off chance that it might reach her ears:

*With the other women you mock me and don't think, my lady,*

*why I cut such an odd figure whenever I look on your beauty.*

*Love, when he finds me close to you, grows so emboldened, so confident*

*that he strikes down my cowering spirits--*

*killing some, driving others out,*

*so that Love alone remains to regard you.*

*Yes, I'm transformed but not so much that I can't feel my outcast senses' torment.*

Dante admitted to some confusing expressions like Love killing all spirits save the one of sight. This idea, these images, this profusion of the heart however extreme were beyond the pale of anyone who wasn't a faithful follower of Love such as himself. The cult of Love! For those like him, no explanations were necessary. So any clarification on his part would be futile to some and superfluous to others.

Instead, another powerful thought struck him, remained and plagued him, self-addressed in the second person:

"Since you assume such a ridiculous appearance whenever you're near this lady—why do you still try to see her?"

Good question! an imaginary shrink might say.

If I were Dante's shrink, I'd ask him:_____.

His internal examiner continued: "If *she* asked you the same question and assuming you have all your wits about you, what would you say?"

His response right away:

"As soon as your wondrous beauty befalls

my eyes, the desire to see you is so powerful that it slays all objections. Past sufferings, humiliations, transformations, tears cannot restrain me."

The poetry:

...that which opposes my desire to see her dies in my mind when I

happen to see my bella gioia —beautiful joy-- and, when I'm near her,

I hear Love say: "Run if you fear death!"

My face mirrors the color of my heart which, trembling again, looks for support and,

in this intoxicated state, the  stones seem to shout, "Die!"


My     nickname(s)     for     my     love     is

_____.


Now the great poet establishes himself at the level of the gods by defining a new sin:

Whosoever sees me like this and doesn't try to comfort me with even the slightest show of grief, sins!

grief which your mocking slays is aroused

by the dead powers of my eyes which, in turn, desire
their own death.

Back down to earth, seemingly on the road to
recovery, the poet decided to make four statements
about his condition he'd not put forth before.

First—often he grieved when he pictured the
sorry state to which Love had reduced him.

Second—many times without warning Love
assailed him so suddenly and so completely that the
sole thought that remained in all his life was the one
that spoke of his lady.

Third—when the Battle of Love waged inside
of him like this, it propelled him to go all pale and
see that lady, believing that the sight of her would
protect him, forgetting what happened to him
whenever he approached such kindness.

Fourth—not only had such sights of her
failed to protect him, they defeated the little life
remaining to him.

On the mend enough to understand that his
three sonnets addressed to Beatrice revealed quite
enough of his sorry state, he resolved to say no

more about it and find new material of a nobler nature.

Widen his horizon! One work in the hopper, move on to the next!

But just as he was about to turn a new leaf, his lovesick appearance—deathly pale, hair sticking up, clothes threadbare, eyes glassy and distant— about which he could do little in a short period of time, came to the attention of many, and just as many had divined his heart's secret. Especially this jovial group of women he'd come upon--chatting, laughing, having a merry time.

Mid-afternoon coffee klatch? Lovers of songs and ballads? They knew the workings of his heart [xxiv]'cause each one had been present at one or more of the spectacles he made of himself in the Beloved's presence. He was just passing by when the ladies turned toward him, one calling out:

"Salve, Dante!"

She had a charming way about her so he approached. When he saw that Beatrice wasn't among them, he was heartened and greeted the women accordingly, bowing his head:

"Ladies, what can I do for you?" Debonair Dante, out to please.

That same pleasant woman turned her eyes to him.

"Dante, we were wondering--to what end do you love that lady of yours, seeing you can't withstand the sight of her? We're curious because the goal of such a love must certainly be novel."

Women of ends not necessarily of means. Women who had at one time or another consummated their own affairs of the heart, some successfully, some with pain.

The other women turned to him—eyes widening, lips parting slightly, smiling hesitantly--in expectation of his reply.

"The goal used to be to get this lady in question to say hello to me. Perhaps you know her? In that consisted the end of all my desires. But since she decided to deny it to me, my master, Love--eternal thanks be to him!--has placed all my joy in something that can't fail me."

The women huddled, spoke together. What couldn't possibly fail this guy and make him happy: self-love? some sadomasochist? Just as sometimes rain falls mixed with beautiful snow, sighs issued from them.

That same light-hearted lady, sort of a spokesperson said:

"We beg you, for the life of us we can't figure out where this joy of yours resides."

"In those words that praise my lady."

The same pleasant lady shot back:

"But if you were telling the truth, when you wrote to her describing your condition, you had some other agenda in mind." That is, all the while he'd said and written that he was imploring her for Pity, he was really in quest of her greeting.

Feeling ashamed, Dante began to move away, saying to himself: "How can I have written or spoken otherwise since complete bliss resides in words of praise of my lady."

That's noble--speak and write not of yourself but of someone else!

It was through this group of good-hearted ladies that Dante at least for the moment discovered new material: adopt as his manner and subject of speaking and writing—forever—whatsoever smacked of this *gentilissima.*

But after thinking it over for some time, he decided he'd undertaken subject matter too lofty. She was unattainable, beyond praise, so he didn't dare pick up his pen. For days he felt the desire to write but couldn't, fearing beginning.

Our great Dante, at the point of desiring to write words of praise of Beatrice—Writers' Block!

My bliss that can't fail me is_____.

So there he was, walking down a long road beside the clear Arno [xxv] when the desire arose in him to write again.

"But how can I go about it?" he asked himself.

Perhaps the steady, soothing burble and splash of his town's river allowed the poet to divine that his words would last as long as the river, as long as men and women longed to love and be loved. For he was about to compose one of his best-loved poems, proving that so-called writer's block may not be that at all, rather it augurs a fresh new start, a creation from deep down to the heights of heaven.

He didn't jump at the first words that came to him but a bit later on concluded:

"Yes, I'll sing her praises but not directly. Instead, I'll write to other women and in the second person"—a device frowned on by book editors now. To further swell his heart at a safe, omniscient distance, he'd direct his words not just to any women but to women *che sono gentili.* Lo and behold, his tongue began to wag, his mouth to speak of its own volition, saying:

*"Donne ch'avete intelletto d'amore..."*[xxvi] "Women who understand love..."

He managed with joy to store these words in his memory till he got home then mused on them for days before he began his *canzone* with the riverside phrase. *"Donne ch'avete intelletto d'amore..."* Not that he thought he could exhaust praises of Beatrice but he merely wanted to "talk" which, in turn, could -*"...isfogar la mente-"* "...unburden the mind--" much needed in his case-- experiencing all those centuries ago the therapeutic function of creative composition.

Thinking of her worthiness, Love made

itself felt so sweetly that if courage didn't fail him—

Everyone Would Fall in Love.


Then Dante spoke in the voice and words of an angel addressing the mind of God:

"Lord, on earth exists a marvel in actions that proceeds from a spirit whose light reaches You"-- Dante anticipates the "Paradise" of his *Comedy*— "Heaven lacks no other save for her and every saint asks for her." Anticipating her mortal death a second time. Then Dante enters the persona of God addressing an angel:

"Peace be with you until it's My pleasure to call her, for there's one down there who expects to lose her--" our Dante! — "and so dreads it."

Now my brethren the incontrovertible genius threading the centuries, the fog drifting down on the Arno's surface: the foretelling of his journey through hell—God still speaking, "One who will say in the inferno-

*"O mal nati, io vidi la speranza de' beati."* "O damned souls, I've seen the hope of the *beati.*"

From God back to the poet's heart and mind:

Whosoever aspires to be a *gentil donna* should go and seek her company, for when she walks, Love casts a chill into cold hearts and destroys their every thought. In her company one becomes noble or dies. Her virtue becomes yours because that which she gives saves you and humbles you so that you forget every offense. Are you able to speak to her? You cannot be damned!

Love says of her:

"How can a mortal being be so beautiful and so pure?"

Love does a double-take, gazing at her again and swears that in her person God intended to create something new.

Then the great poet gives up a detail, humanizing Beatrice at least in this part of his song.

"Her color is the paleness of a pearl.[xxvii]"

Then he sent his song on its way:

Canzone, since I raised you from young, plain daughter of Love, wherever you go pray make this request: "Help me find my way for I've been sent to the one whose praises adorn me. Open your heart only to women or a courteous man who will send you straightaway on your path. You'll find

Love with her. Commend me to him, as well you should."

What other idea can possibly emerge from composing a song in praise of her than--

Love.

His *canzone* became known not only among women—Dante Matinee Idol!—but also among men, including his good friend and mentor, Guido Guinizzelli, who, acquiring confidence from Dante's song "beyond my worth," writes humble Dante, requested his definition of Love.

Love and the gentle heart were one and the same —"You can't have one without the other," goes the modern song, just as you can't have reason without a reasoning mind. Lording over Love and the gentle heart was Nature itself which in turn created Love when in a loving mood. Love as King, the heart Love's palace. And in one's heart Love lay dormant sometimes for a longer time, sometimes shorter.

Dante's system of Love works like this:

Let's say your eyes take in a worthy gal or guy with great pleasure.

Desire for that creature is born in the heart, and this desire lingers until Love's spirit is aroused from its sleep.

Dante concludes: This definition of Love holds also for men.

I think Love is_____.

On a roll, he felt the urge to write some more, this time in praise of *questa gentilissima*, showing how Love was awakened through her not only where he lay sleeping but also, miraculously, where he was not. Love borne of his lady's eyes imparted its grace to all she looked on, causing the heart to quake, the face to whiten, forcing down the gaze. All one's defects flashed to mind and— "Aaahh," sighed the poet, and all pride and indignation fled before her.

Tenderness in the original:

*Ogni dolcezza, ogne pensero umile*
*nasce nel core a chi parlar la sente,*
*ond'è laudato chi prima la vide.*
*Quel ch'ella par quando un poco sorride,*
*non si pò dicer nè tenere a mente,*

*sì è novo miracolo e gentile.*

Every sweetness, every humble thought is born in the heart of whoever hears her speak. He who first sees her is blessed.

How she looks when she smiles slightly can't be uttered or grasped by the mind it's such a miracle strange and novel.


A few days after his preoccupation and writing on Love, a real-life event occurred that transported him further away from writing about his sorry state--the death of Beatrice's father, Folco dei Portinari.[xxviii]

Dante goes on to write one of the first obits in Western lit in unique fashion, focusing not on the deceased per se—Folco: prior, banker, founder of the hospital Santa Maria de' Cerchi, where he's buried--but on his daughter Beatrice. We learn about Folco through her, the way the moon is lit by the sun. At the same time, such a double-edged device helps establish Beatrice as a real-life character, for like all men and women born, she had a father.

As it pleased the glorious Lord who didn't refuse death for himself, the man who'd been father to the marvel that was the most gracious Beatrice surely passed into eternal glory. Great men such as Folco and Dante himself could attain eternal glory through Beatrice. The bitter grief she suffered was the sum total of such separations being painful to friends left behind and the fact that there's no closer relationship than a good father's for a good child and a good child's for a good father. And Beatrice was good in the highest degree—thus she was filled with grief most bitter.

He was among the men mourning outside. Knowing that Beatrice would be among the women keeping vigil over her father's corpse, he positioned himself in such a way that he could overhear women who'd witnessed Beatrice weep pathetically emerging from the wake. These words filtered out to him:

"Anyone who sees her weeping would be moved to pity."

Tears of pity drenched Dante's face which he, master of concealment, sought to hide by lifting his hands to his eyes and covering them.

For Dante, eyes were among the first of our salient features.

He could've gone out of view the moment he began to weep but he held out hope to hear more. Which he did. A second cluster of women passed, one mourner saying:

"Who among us can ever be happy again having witnessed that lady speak so piteously?"

A third group of women went by, one remarking:

"This man here weeps exactly as if he'd seen her, as we have."

Another woman of this same group granted his subliminal desire of recognizing him weeping as if he'd seen Beatrice!

"He doesn't seem himself, he's changed so."

Where had she seen him before? That wedding ritual at the new groom's house where he'd broken down?

Dante enriched his obituary with questioning these women and having them respond, employing something like a "Call and Response" device.

"Oh you with humble bearing, your eyes lowered in an expression of grief—where do you come from [doubling up through the rhetorical device, the poet knowing full well from whence they'd come] that your countenance resembles that of pity?" *Pietà* personified with color. "And did you see our gentle lady bathe her face with tears of Love?" Signor Amor weeps! "Since you come from a scene of such profound pity, stay with me awhile and don't conceal the slightest thing about her. I see your eyes full of tears, and I see you leaving so disfigured that my heart trembles."

Lady: "Are you the guy who's oft spoke of our lady only to us? Your voice sounds like his but you look like someone else."

Dante's at least dual personality manifest.

She went on: "And why do you weep so convincingly that you arouse pity in others? Did you see her weep such that you can't conceal your own sorrowful state?"

Responding with "Calls" of their own.

Then the women embraced the poet so that

they joined as one and said:

"Let's weep and go about sadly (he sins who dares to comfort us) for we've heard her speak while she weeps. Pity is so plain on her face that whoever deigns to look at her dies weeping in her presence."

Not only Folco waked but also those of us who picture her in her private moments of grief.

A few days after Folco died, Dante suffered great pain[xxix] in some part of his body—appendicitis? peritonitis? sympathy?—for nine straight days. He lay in bed, paralyzed. On the ninth day, the pain almost unbearable, a thought came to him about his lady which he pondered awhile then his thoughts returned to his frail, sick body--how short life is even if one is healthy. He began to sob and, sighing deeply, said to himself:

"Some day the most gentle Beatrice will die."

This realization sent him reeling, hallucinating strong and vivid like a madman. He shut his eyes and imagined he saw women with disheveled hair, who said to him:

"You, too, will die."

Other faces too horrible to look at appeared and said: "You are dead."

He didn't know where he was. He thought he saw those horrible women walking down a street directly toward him, some weeping, some wailing who darted flames of sorrow. The sun gradually darkened and the stars came out, and the sun and the stars were weeping. Birds flying through the air fell to the ground. The earth shook. Then a pale man with a hoarse voice appeared and said:

"Haven't you heard? Your *mirabile donna* has departed from this life!"

He began to weep piteously not solely in his imagination but with real tears which bathed his hot cheeks. He looked up at the sky and saw, resembling manna raining down, a multitude of angels preceded by a very white cloud. The angels sang:

*"Osanna in excelsis!"* xxx

His heart in which resided so much love said: "It's true: our lady lies dead."

His false imaginings lead him to see the

Beloved's body that had sheltered the most worthy and blessed soul. Other women covered her head with a veil. Her face filled with humble aspect said:

"I'm seeing the onset of peace."

Dante's goal of attaining peace is reached through Beatrice in death. Seeing her this way filled him with such humility that he called on death:

"Sweetest death, come to me and don't be cruel considering where you've just been. Now come to me for I desire you, you see I already wear your color."

After he'd seen all the sorrowful tasks customarily performed on the bodies of the dead, Dante returned to his cryptic room where his hallucinations continued, his gaze turned up at the heavens. So intense was his imagining that, weeping, he cried out in believable voice:

"O most beautiful soul, how blessed is he who sees you!"

The compassionate lady of tender years

caring for him ^xxxi, said to be a sister, believing that his weeping and impassioned outcries stemmed from his pain, and seeing his eyes full of pity, and hearing his hysterical words--she grew fearful and began to cry. Other women in the room all this time, noticing the young woman's tears, made her leave then approached his bed. Believing that young Dante was dreaming, one woman said:

"Don't sleep!" Another: "Why do you despair!" interrupting his reverie just as he was about to say: "O Beatrice be blessed!" He'd just managed, "O Beatrice..." when rousing himself he opened his eyes and realized he'd been delusional. Though he'd uttered her name, his sobs may have broken it up, so the women in the room may not have understood. Only his heart had heard it and so, feeling ashamed, by some admonition of Love, he turned to them and looked them in the eye, his pallor that of death.

One woman implored the others:

"Let's comfort him." Another woman: "What were you afraid of?" Several together more than once: "What did you see that weakened you so?"

Feeling somewhat comforted and his head clearing by the minute, he said:

"I'll tell you what happened to me."

And he went on to tell them all he'd seen, omitting only the name of *la gentillissima,* that most noble lady, the most gracious one, the untranslatable.

Finally, alone, every sorrow consumed, he looked up at the high heaven and exclaimed:

*"Beato, anima bella, chi te vede!"* "Beautiful soul, blessed is he who sees you."

After he recovered quite peacefully from his illness of nine days and his grotesque reveries of Beatrice's death which, naturally, led to the prospect of his own, he was sitting "in a certain place"— piazza? inn?—meditating, when he felt a tremor in his heart as if he was in her presence. Sure enough a vision of Love came to him. He was all aglow for he was coming from a place where his lady had been and had acquired some of her aspect. Love embedded himself in Dante's heart and said, laughing at every word:

"Bless the day I took you captive because

you're obliged to." In other words--You owe me!

Dante's heart was so happy it didn't seem like his own. It spoke to him in the Language of Love whereupon a gentlewoman known for her great beauty approached--his best friend Guido Cavalcanti's lady named Giovanna. On account of her great beauty some people dubbed her *Primavera,* Springtime, and, trailing behind her, was *la mirabile* Beatrice.[xxxii] Love said to him in his heart:

"The one in front is called *Primavera* solely because of the way she comes first in line for I inspired the giver of her name to call her Primavera because she will come first—*prima verrà.* Also, Giovanna's name signifies 'she will come' because Giovanna comes from Giovanni, that is, John the Baptist, who preceded the True Light, saying: "*Ego vox clamantis in deserto: parate viam Domini,*" "I am the voice of one crying in the wilderness, prepare ye the way of the Lord."

Love said to him:

"If you think about it carefully, Beatrice would be called Love, she resembles me so."

Then the Poet paused to provide an early

instance of Literary Criticism, using his own work as model.

His words described Amor, or Love, as "him," and we saw Love "coming," indicating movement through space. And Love spoke and laughed as if he were a man and possessed a body. Well, any reader of his deserving of having all doubt dispelled should know that Love is not a physical substance as well as an intellectual substance. Rather, Love is an *accident* of substance, existing as a result of poetic license. Such poetic license in behalf of poets writing in the vernacular, including himself, relied on history. In ancient times, there were no "love poets"; that is, poets writing of love in the vernacular.

Only lettered poets writing in Latin spoke of love, such work aimed at the educated classes, clergy and aristocracy--love privileged. But then, approaching his own time, the 13th Century, poets began writing of love in the vernacular, that is, Italian, because women had difficulty comprehending Latin when there was nothing really complicated about love. Imagine if our modern *50 Shades of Gray* had been written in ye olde

Englishe—how many fewer women could have comprehended and reveled in it! The vernacular was invented in order to speak of love in a straightforward, accessible way. Those writers of Latin possessed poetic license to personify the inanimate. Virgil, classical Latin poet who will become his guide through the *Inferno*, in his *Aeneid* says that Juno, goddess hostile to the Trojans, speaks to Aeolus god of the winds. And Lucan addresses Rome as if the eternal city were a living, breathing thing: "Much, Rome, do you nevertheless owe to civic arms". In Ovid's *The Remedy of Love,* Love speaks in the skin and mouth of a human being: *"Bella michi, video, bella parantur, ait."* "Wars against me, I see, wars are preparing, he says." Therefore, poetic license of the classical poets should also be granted to poets of the vernacular, in the process placing himself in the context of literary history. But Dante, a perfectionist, provided an essential caveat: yes, write of love in the vernacular but with "strict rules" so that not anyone like today who picks up a pen or taps a computer key or reads a so-called poem in a café is a writer.

Vernacular poets should have a *reason* for

writing about love, for great embarrassment would ensue for those who've written things in the dress of an image or rhetorical figure and later on asked to explain the true meaning of his or her words, and cannot.

Dante's progress of writing about his lovesick persona to subjects outside of himself, especially words of praise of Beatrice, vaulted her into widespread favor. When she walked down a street, people ran up to see her. Tongues stammered then grew mute. She went about crowned and clothed in humility, unaffected by what she saw and heard. Her modesty filled one's heart so that it became the other's, such that he dared not raise his head nor return her greeting. From her lips issued a gentle, loving spirit that slipped into men's souls and whispered—

"Ahhh."

Through her eyes she displayed wonder and sweetness and filled her admirers with such modesty that many were unable to find the words to describe her, leaving it solely for Dante to do so. His intoxication of her, rather than inhibiting his talent, enriched it. She seemed like something sent from heaven to earth in order to demonstrate a miracle. Through her, every woman received honor. For any doubting Thomases, just as many could testify that it was so. Her popularity brought him the greatest joy.

Word of mouth was Dante's social media and the way his work got around.

After she passed by, some said: "That's no ordinary woman, she's one of the most beautiful angels."

Others said: "She's a wonder! Blessed be the Lord able to perform such miracles."

Here's how I'd describe my love:_____.

One day he stepped back and went over what he'd said about his lady in his last two sonnets. He hadn't spoken about the effects she'd had on him at that time. Praise also had to reflect the praiser, again like the sun illuminating the moon. A poem of 14 lines provided enough space and time to tell how open he felt to her influence, how her virtue affected him, how for so long Love had held him in its thrall. Just as Amor had been harsh to him, now he dwelled gently in his heart. So that when Amor took away his strength, causing his spirits to take flight, his frail soul felt such sweetness that his face paled and his spirits went around calling on his lady to grant him grace. This happened wherever she saw him.

*"Quomodo sedet sola civitas plena populo! facta est quasi vidua domina gentium."*
"How the city full of people sits solitary! How has she become a widow that was great among nations!"—Lamentations of Jeremiah 1:1

He was in the process of composing a song using the above scripture when the Lord of Justice called this most gracious lady to His glory under the banner of the Blessed Virgin Mary[xxxiii], Whose name always issued from Beatrice's lips with the greatest reverence.

Death snatched the Beloved away so soon upon her public favor and his progress at rehabilitation[xxxiv].

Though at the moment he would've liked to write about her departure, it wasn't his intention for three reasons:

First, if we consider the preface of their little book, her death was never intended to be included. Since she'd already died before he began transcribing the crux of a New Life, perhaps her death a second time in the process of such transcription was too much for him to bear.

Second, even if it had been his intention, the language at his command was insufficient. He simply didn't have the words.

Third, supposing that the first and second reasons didn't exist, it'd be improper to deal with her death 'cause dealing with it would entail praising himself, a thing exceedingly blameworthy in the person who does it. Self-praise being tantamount to existence while, without her, he was devoid of self. He'd leave the topic of Beatrice's earthly demise to other writers. Omg! Dante divined me centuries in advance! Nevertheless, since the number $9^{xxxv}$ cropped up many times among the preceding words, and since this number played a major role in her departure, it was fitting to say a few words concerning it:

"According to the Arabian, Syrian and Christian calendars, she died on the 9th day of the 9th month in the year of Our Lord 1290, during which, according to St. Thomas, the perfect number 10 appeared 9 times. Another reason why this number was in such harmony with her is this: according to Ptolemy[xxxvi] and Christian truths, there are 9 heavens that move and, according to sound astrological wisdom, these heavens affect the earth below in proportion to their workings among themselves—that number was congenial to her in order to make us understand that at her conception all nine moving heavens were in perfect relation one to the other. This is one reason but pondering it more subtly, and in accordance with infallible truth, this number was she herself, by similitude. I mean, the number three is the root of nine because without the intervention of any other number, three creates nine by itself, as we plainly see that three times three makes nine. Therefore, if three by itself is a factor of nine and the factor of miracles is also three—that is, Father, Son and the Holy Ghost Who are three in one—that lady was accompanied by the number nine to make us understand that she *was* a nine, that is, a miracle, whose root is the miraculous Trinity.

"Perhaps a more subtle person could see in this a more subtle explanation but this is the one that I see and which pleases me most."

After she departed from this world, Florence was left a widow stripped of dignity.

In addition to being the Beloved, largely amorphous, not once fully described, like a mist hovering above their river appearing then disappearing then appearing again in the same way for centuries, as much as anything an act of faith-- Beatrice is also principality, their city's departed mistress. Still, we come to know the giant Dante through her.

The Lover still weeping over her wrote of their city's barren condition to the princes of the land[xxxvii], taking for his beginning the above words from the Lamentations of Jeremiah, those princes unaware that he was really referring to his Beloved.

What good outcome did he have in mind writing to these influential men? Declaring a national holiday would have been unlikely as, outside of her family and a few friends, she was known solely to him.

His citation from Jeremiah would serve as preface to the new material that followed. And if anyone should reproach him for not continuing the quote, he'd say that from the outset his intention was to write in the vernacular while those continuing words were in Latin. In so doing he pleased his friend Guido to whom he was writing, whose wish also was that he, Dante, write solely in the vernacular.

Late now in his memory of their little book, the poet attempted to bestow on the Beloved the unbridled gift of moving on, leaving her in eternal peace. He'd do this through his greatest strength, his poetry, and its subject would be an abstraction, sorrow itself.

Between salty, streaming tears and words of sorrow was the relief wrought by his mind and imagination.

Sorrow's vehicle[xxxviii] was a *canzone* in which he'd sing tearfully of her through whom so much grief had destroyed his soul. He'd sing without a soul, for his soul, like Florence and Beatrice, was stripped of its elements—his widowed soul! leaving him with his art. His song must also appear widow-like, so he decided to divide it up in prose description before he transformed it to the poetry. In this way, also, the women could comprehend it more readily. His long, doleful song had three parts—

First: introductory, which begins *Li occhi dolenti per pietà del core*...The eyes grieving through pity for the heart... And how weeping, grieving and suffering left defeated, tearless eyes: now he must vent his grief, blow it down the centuries, grief which little by little leads to his own death. And he remembered how he spoke gladly about his lady "to you, *donne gentili,* gracious ladies, you alone." His singular *bella gioia* transformed to all women of tender heart. *Donne ch'avete intelleto d'amore.* Lamenting, he'd tell them how she suddenly ascended to Heaven, leaving Love behind to grieve with him.

Second: he backtracks and speaks of the ascending Beatrice, the one who'd gone to heaven, to the realm where the angels enjoy peace.

"...having left you, ladies, not by a chill or fever like others, but solely through her *benignitate...*"

Here's how she passed from the earthly to the heavenly realm: her humility's light pierced the heavens with such force that the Lord marveled, and a sweet desire moved Him to summon *tanta salute.* He brought her up to Him because the offensive life down here wasn't worthy of *gentil cosa.*

Once shed of her form, her gentle soul now lived in a worthy place. Whoever spoke of her and didn't lament possessed an impenetrable heart of stone.

An evil heart didn't own the wit to figure her out and so lacked the urge to weep from grief. But sadness came and the desire to die from weeping. The soul's consolation was stripped in anyone who pictured what she was like and how she left us. His sighs filled him with anguish every time the image arose of she who broke his heart. The urge to die taking hold in him drained the color in his face. Trembling from the pain, shame drove away everyone from him.

Alone now, weeping in his lament, he called

Beatrice, saying: "Are you dead now?" The virtuous dead hear. Though dead, she consoled him. Should anyone hear him, he would also grieve. What his life's been like since she left no tongue can tell. And so, ladies, he addresses them, even if he tried, he couldn't say what he'd become. A life so base that when anyone saw his pallid face, they said: "I abandon you." But his lady knew who he was, and he held out hope that she would show him *merzede,* grace, mercy.

Third: he beseeches the song itself--

"Pitiful song, go now in tears and find once more ladies and maidens

to whom your sister songs used to bring joy. And you, daughter of sadness,

go now disconsolately and stay with them."


A man came to him who according to degrees of friendship was second after poet Guido Cavalcanti, a blood relation of *la gloriosa,* said to be a brother, he couldn't have been closer.

Ah! so that's was how he may have known about Beatrice, through her brother. They'd been close friends from boyhood through their teens to early manhood, playing on the cobbled streets under the sun, visiting one another's homes when it rained, later on going out together in the piazza taking coffees, smoking cigars, reading and listening to poems and songs. At every stage, Dante may have caught glimpses of her, and she of him.

After they had spoken awhile, the conversation turned to a request for Dante to write something about a lady who was dead. The friend didn't say who the lady was but disguised his words as if he were speaking of someone other than his sister who'd recently died.  He may have felt that requesting lofty words about one's sister was vain. Or this brother knew Dante's true feelings for her, had witnessed how he grew pale in her company, swoon from a glance or a nod from her and also was cognizant of Screen Ladies #1 & #2. Dante, aware of his friend's deception, went along with the idea of writing such a stand-in poem, a sonnet by which he'd camouflage his own sorrow by making it the brother's.

Dante--medieval Cyrano de Bergerac!

He addressed the *cor gentili,* the gracious hearts, to come listen to his sighs-

Dante at this age a young man full of sighs—for pity demanded it, sighs that issued disconsolately which, if it not for them, he'd die of grief...Hear those sighs calling on *la mia donna gentil* who had gone on to a life worthy of her virtue...

But before he sent off his sonnet, he thought about the quality of his friend—his words sold him short, were at base *povero...e nudo,* poor and naked. By way of revision he composed an ode of two stanzas with the slight difference of one word: "my." One stanza calls her "my lady" and one doesn't. Then he sent off the sonnet and the ode, saying that both had been written by his friend.

The ode begins, *Quantunque volte, lasso!...*

Every time, alas! I recall I'll never again see the lady for whom I grieve so, such great

sorrow gathers 'round my heart by my sorrowful mind that it says: "Soul, why don't you leave?"

Dante's Bergeracean ode went on to the poet calling on death *"Vieni a me,"* to come to him as a sweet, gentle repose such that he begrudged whoever dies. To *Pietà*, Pity, turned his desires since that day when--here comes that one telling word difference—"my" lady was stricken by death's cruelty, the pleasure of her beauty leaving our sight transformed to a great spiritual beauty spreading the light of life throughout the heavens, a light of love that greets the angels and moves their subtle, lofty intellects to marvel—that's how gracious it is.

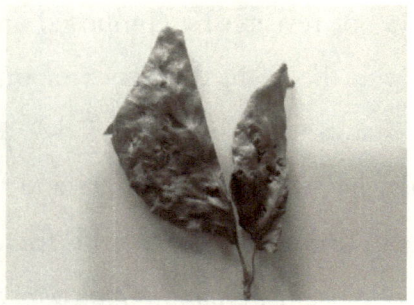

Angel-leaf construction-Anthony Valerio

Then Dante was sitting in some place having in mind the light of love that was his lady greeting the angels in heaven. It was exactly one year to the day of the Beloved's death, the conventional time of mourning over: women shedding their black, the dead having reached at least the first of their destinations, widows and widowers free to find new love. Dante was drawing an angel on "carte tavolette,"[xxxix] parchments six-inches squared used by beginners in drawing exercises, and happened to turn his head and see alongside him a group of men *...li quali si convenia fare onore...*deserving of honor. Progressive public servants of the ilk of Folco? Art school faculty? They'd been watching him draw for awhile, he was told later on. Dante stood up and said:

"Someone was here with me just now, that's why I was lost in thought."

This guy some odd ball? "Someone was with me..." The illustrious men left, and Dante returned to drawing his angel.[xl]

"Why don't I write a poem celebrating the first anniversary of her death in honor of the men who'd come and watched me draw an angel," he thought. The poem would have two different opening quatrains, both beginning, *"Era venuta..."* One difference: in the second quatrain he'd tell when that lady had entered his senses.

First opening, one-line medieval Haiku:

There'd come to my mind the noble lady

who because of her worth the Lord on High placed in the Heaven of Humility, where Mary is.

The second, or alternative, opening:

There'd come to my mind that noble lady for whom Love weeps—at that moment when her worth caused you gentlemen to look at what I was doing. Love who felt her in my mind awakened in my ravaged heart and said to my sighs: "Go!" Sighs that issued forth with the greatest pain said as they came: ...*Oi nobile intelletto, oggi fa l'anno che nel ciel salisti.* O noble intellect, today marks the first year since you ascended to heaven.

The anniversaries of my loved ones are:_____.

Nostalgia occupied him now, for then he was in a place that called up times past where he'd beheld Beatrice. He was intensely pensive, beset by images, sounds and feeling of sadness that must have made his face look terribly distressed. No one must see, so he raised his eyes—was anyone watching?—and, leaning out from her window, was *una gentile donna,* a kind lady young and beautiful staring down at him with compassion, taking in the suffering on his face, penetrating the nature of his conflicted soul. All pity of all time gathered in her! If he couldn't arouse pity in one woman, he'd do so in another. Since someone miserable who saw another showing compassion toward him was readily moved to tears, tears began to fall and overwhelm him.

The fear arose in him of showing this woman his wretched state. He stood up and fled, saying:

"Surely Love lives in this woman who makes me go around weeping like this."

Whenever this Lady in the Window saw him, her face wondrously took on a pitying expression and turned pale, almost like a look of Love, so that the Lover frequently recalled the Beloved, who displayed a similar pallor.

Certainly, many times, unable to weep or soothe his sorrow, he'd go in search of this compassionate lady whose very appearance inspired in him an urge to weep, though not in her presence.

But then his sight of the Lady of Compassion began to bring him much pleasure—not a very positive turn of events in this poet's case—and in time tormented him and lowered the opinion he had of himself. So he often cursed the vain nature of his eyes, saying to them: "You used to reduce everybody who looked on your pitiful state to tears, and now because this young, beautiful girl shows you kindness, you forget. But her eyes turned to you merely because she grieves for the *gloriosa donna* you used to lament." His eyes' lack of purpose gave him pause and frightened him. He feared the face of the woman who oft now looked on them with kindness. "Never forget the lady who has died till you yourself die"--so said his heart, then it sighed.

Then it happened that the sight of this compassionate lady inspired a new frame of mind in him such that he considered her a person he liked too well. He thought of her in these terms: "She's a kind, lovely, prudent lady who has appeared by the grace of Love so that I may find some peace."

Finally, peace--but peace in the guise of a woman other than the Beloved.

Often, he thought of the Lady in the Window even more lovingly. His heart, Love's reasoning, concurred. Going this far he had second thoughts, more rational ones, and said to himself:

"God, what's going on with these thoughts which attempt to console me in a vile way and hardly allow me to think differently."

Peace comes as a perplexing stranger. Yet another thought said to him:

"You've suffered such tribulation, why do you not want to withdraw from such bitterness?" Take a time out! Be good to yourself! His thought continued: "You see that this is an inspiration of Love, who presents his desire to us and has as its origin the eyes of the lady who showed herself so compassionate to us."

Another one of the Poet's internal battles was underway. In this one, words uttered in her favor proved victorious. A final gracious thought found its way into the poetics of this section— Beatrice evermore.

... gracious is this thought because it speaks of her, of Beatrice,

coming frequently to live awhile inside of me, and speaks melodiously of Love,

and this thought talks the heart into surrendering.

Then a conversation took place between his soul and his heart.

The soul to the heart: "Who is this one who comes with consolation to the mind, possessing great strength, permitting not another thought to remain?"

The heart to the soul: "O pensive soul, this is a new spirit of love that brings its desires to me, his life and his worth arose from the eyes of that pitying lady so perturbed by our suffering."

Against that adversary of reason there arose one day about the hour of nones, between noon and three, ecclesiastically, the hours in which Jesus suffered his agony and was crucified, a vivid vision, the poet's penultimate.

The glorious Beatrice was dressed in her blood-red dress in which she first appeared before his eyes, when they were nine. Continuing his nostalgic bent, the closer he came to the end of transcribing their little book, the further back he traveled. *Vita nova* is like a circle rolling down through the centuries. He conjured up the times he'd seen her, in sequence. Here Dante does what good prose writers after him have done--once past the point of no return, they review some, so that the reader can recall that which the author wishes. Yes, round 'n' round the May Pole, holding on to their streamers; skipping, laughing. And then nine years later, she approached dressed in white and turned her eyes toward him and nodded her greeting. In his Room of Tears, how could he forget his first vision of her as she lay supine in Love's arms and, hesitantly, ate his heart? In their small chapel he couldn't withstand his eyes directly affixed on her standing/sitting/genuflecting/making the Sign of the Cross--her head veiled, in a forward pew. Walking along a certain street, she denied him her hello--it seemed an eternity he'd waited for it, an eternity deprived. At that wedding ritual of the bride's first dinner at the groom's house —"Why have we come to see these women?" he'd asked his trustworthy friend—and he could feel still the tremor in his heart spread throughout his body, bracing himself against the frescoed wall and then raising his eyes and beholding her. In his mind he thought he saw her lying dead, other women covering her with a veil.

Finally, the time he saw her come as Christ had, second after the Baptist, trailing behind Guido's lady, *Primavera,* Spring, the first seen.

The rhyme and reason for this recapitulation was repentance for his heart wandering for days in the direction of the Lady in the Window[xli]—how dare he!—and to have Beatrice return in her glory through the power of memories of her in chronological order. In this way, similar bouts of errant desire were dispelled forever and all thoughts for all time reverted to her. His sighs served as proof of how intensely he thought of her with a shameful heart. Bursting forth, these sighs echoed what was said in his heart: "Beatrice" and how she departed from this world out of the meaning of her name. Such anguish followed that he forgot what he was thinking and where he was. Their little memory book was approaching its end on a note of disorientation on the Lover's part. A circle whirling dervish-like. Once soothed tears flowed again, his eyes transformed to two objects that could only weep. Purple rings formed around them, the way they did around eyes of the long suffering. This was payback for his errant ways, his roving eye. From then on, no one could ever look into them with similar intention.

During the season when pilgrims[xlii] traveled to Rome in order to view the blessed image that Jesus Christ left of His beautiful face[xliii], Whom his gracious lady Beatrice beheld in glory, they passed through their town down a street he knew so well, the one where that gracious lady had been born, lived and died. They seemed lost in thought, provoking a thought in him:

"These pilgrims seem to me to come from distant parts and most likely have never heard tell of my lady"—pilgrims as distributors of the writer's work—their thoughts centered on matters other than local ones, perhaps on friends back home. Dante said further to himself:

"If they were from some nearby place, they'd appear upset when walking through the center of this sorrowful city." Sheer knowledge of her would spread and infuse like pollen flying through the nearby air in search of its counterpart. Her death had left her moving shadow. "If I could detain them awhile, I'd make them weep before they leave this city because I'd speak words that would make them cry."

Dante Tearjerker!


After these Pilgrims passed out of sight, he wrote a sonnet which in order for it to provoke even more pity Madonna-like, he addressed the absent Pilgrims directly, beginning: O pilgrims lost in thought... Pilgrims understood in both the broad and restricted sense. Broad: anyone outside his/her native area. Strict: anyone not on the way or returning from the House of St. James church of Santiago of Compostella, burial place of St. James[xliv] in Galicia, Spain, pointed out by a star in the $9^{th}$ century. It should also be known, Dante went on, that those who travel in the service of our Lord can be called Palmers if they travel overseas and bring back palm leaves. Called pilgrims if they travel to the church in Galicia because the tomb of St. James is more distant from his home than those of the other apostles. And called *romei* if they go to Rome.

The poem:

If you (Pilgrims) stop for a brief repose and

listen, my sighing heart assures me that

you will weep while departing from this city.
It has lost its Beatrice, its blessedness, its beatitude—

and the words that can be said of her have
the power to make anyone weep.


Then two gentlewomen commissioned some
poems of his, as he was gaining popularity very close
to the end of their book's last words. Eager to
spread his work, he sought to comply and, in order
to comply more respectfully, resolved to write
something new--yes, something about his condition—
back to that, accompanied by the earlier sonnet
which, as we have seen, begins: *Venite a intendere li
sospiri miei...* Come hear my sighs...

Had these gentlewomen also lost a loved
one, a relative? spouse?


His new sonnet for these women and the last
one transcribed began—*Oltre la spera che più larga
gira...*placing Beatrice now and forever beyond the
sphere of the widest orbit, in the Empyrean. The

poet was left with a sigh issuing from his heart on which love bestowed a new intelligence that drove that very sigh ever upward. Reaching its desirous destination, his sigh saw a lady, radiant, receiving honors through which the pilgrim spirit could see her. But when he reported back, subtly, to his grieving heart which bid it speak, the poet did not comprehend.

*So io che parla di quella gentile,*

*però che spesso ricorda Beatrice, sì ch'io lo 'ntendo ben, donne mie care.*

I know he speaks of that noble lady because he often mentions Beatrice, so that I understand well, my dear ladies.


Save for one last miraculous vision, *Vita nova* had come to its end. Since it would always be written beforehand, etched in memory, a matter of the unnamed poet transcribing its crux, you could go back and read it over & over, ad infinitum. Thus it remains, no less, no more. In his last vision, *io vide cose...,* he saw things that made him resolve to speak no further of this *benedetta* until the day--

...I can speak of her in a more worthy

manner, toward which I'm

striving as hard as I possibly can, which she well knows. If it should

please the One through Whom all things live that I should live a few more years,

*io spero di dicer di lei quello che mai non fue detto d'alcuna.*

I hope to write of her that which no man has ever written of a woman.

After that may it please the Lord of Courtesy that his soul ascend—the poet rises! —to behold the glory of its lady, that is, of that blessed Beatrice, who in glory gazes upon the face of Him *qui est per Omnia secula benedictus.* Who is blessed through all eternity.

# Notes

[i] A word about the title–alternately titled Vita *nova,* *Vita Nuova, La Vita Nuova.* We do not have the actual title as Dante wrote it, if one at all. In the very first paragraph, the work's proemio, Dante writes *vita nova,* as good a title as we have. Even doubly tantalizing is the idea that what we have is only the gist or crux of a *libello,* little book of his memory, before which very little was written: what was the whole from which this summary was culled and what was the very little that was written. We can only imagine. About the title, from Dante Gabriel Rossetti's translation (1848;1861) into English. "The adjective *Nuovo, nuova,* or *Novello, novella,* literally *New,* is often used by Dante and other early writers in the sense of *young.* This has induced some editors of the *Vita Nuova* to explain the title as meaning *Early Life.* I should be glad on some accounts to adopt this supposition, as everything is a gain which increases clearness to the modern reader; but on consideration I think the more mystical interpretation of the words, as *New Life* (in reference to that revulsion of his being which Dante so minutely describes as having occurred simultaneously with his first sight of Beatrice), appears the primary one, and therefore the most necessary to be given in a translation. The probability may be that both were meant, but this I cannot convey."

Publishing history: "The compilation of the VN can be dated between 1291 and 1294. Some of the lyrics are way older than this: Dante re-contextualizes them in the VN. As for all other Dantean works, we don't have an autograph. The first manuscript of the VN that we possess is the Martelli 12 of the Biblioteca Laurenziana in Florence. It was produced in Gubbio in the first quarter of the 14th century (Dante is probably still alive!). We have a total of 43 codices, or manuscripts, including two in Giovanni Boccaccio's hand. The first printed edition was published in Florence by Sermantelli in 1576 (very very late). Until the philologically correct editions of the $20^{th}$ century, people used to read copies of Boccaccio's version, which took most of the prose out of the main text and put them in the margins. In fact, Boccaccio considered them marginalia to the poems (he even gives a short explanation of why he thinks so in the two manuscripts he himself copies)."-- Francesco Marco Aresu, Assistant Professor of Italian, Department of Romance Languages and Literatures, Wesleyan University.

[ii] "Chapter divisions is a modern invention (19th century) and there is no evidence Dante used them. The narrative division proceeds by poems or situations, etc."—Professor Giuseppe Mazzotta, Yale University.

The early Dante biographer & poet Giovanni Boccaccio states that this first meeting between Beatrice and Dante took place at the May Day Feast, early May, of 1274.

[iii] heaven of light: the sun. In Dante's adoption of the Ptolemaic system of astronomy, there were nine revolving concentric heavens or spheres, immovable

Earth at the center. In each of the first seven is fixed one of the planets which revolves with it. They are, counting outward from the Earth, the Moon, Mercury, Venus, the Sun, Mars, Jupiter, Saturn. The eighth heaven is that of the Fixed Stars, the ninth the crystalline Primum Mobile, and outside of all is the motionless tenth heaven, the Empyrean, this last also immovable and divine, the seat of God. Since the heaven of the sun had almost completed nine of its circles since his birth, Dante calculates that he was almost nine years old when he met Beatrice.

iv twelfth of a degree: it was believed that the Fixed Stars moved west to east one degree every 100 years, or one-twelfth of a degree in eight years and four months—thus Dante calculates Beatrice's age when they first met. The boy was slightly older than the girl. This motion of the stars in relation to the earth is now known as the Precession of the Equinoxes.

v the glorious lady of his mind: names for Beatrice include *questa gentilissima, questa cortesissima, la mia beatitudine, bella gioia* which I have left in the original, untranslatable.

vi her dress: medieval Dantist Francesco Flamini states that she wore a girdle around her waist and probably a wreath of flowers on her head.

vii vital spirit: it's often written that Dante took from Albertus Magnus (pre 1200-1280) his categories of the three central spirits: vital, animal, and natural.

Dante isolates, animates and interconnects these spirits, making them palpable, dynamic forces of character. Perhaps an early holistic approach to sensory perception & reception. On *spirit,* Professor Kenneth McKenzie's note: An intermediary, a sort of fluid substance, was supposed to exist between the soul and the body, partaking of the nature of both and unable to exist without them; this intermediary substance was supposed to have actual physical substance, and was called *spiritus or spirit.* By means of it the soul governed the organs of the body. The soul of man is single but has three forms: vegetative, sensitive, rational; so also the *spiritus* is single and has three forms or manifestations: originating in the heart as the "vital" spirit, it becomes "natural" in the liver, and "animal" (belonging to the mind, *animus)* in the brain"

The spirits of sight, a major focus of Dante's, were for him actual fluid substances which moved freely, sometimes even leaving their owner.

[viii] "drew on Homer's *Iliad*": *Iliad* xxiv.258-9. Dante knew Homer from his reading of Aristotle's Latin translation.

[ix] greeted him: the first time he records he heard her voice.

[x] marvelous vision: the first of three which placement throughout the work gives it balance and equal divisions marked by flights of fancy.

xi About Dante's poetic apprenticeship in *Vita Nuova*, Professor Giuseppe Mazzotta states: "It is a matter of opinion, in the absence of certain proof, that Dante's apprenticeship, at least his technical training as an autodidact poet, had taken place before and kept taking place during his writing of the VN: he is credited by some, myself included, with translating into Italian sonnets the French epic, *Roman de la Rose.*"

xii **"sonnets"**—"Dante's sonnets in what he called *"Il Fiore"* are a far cry from the "sweet, new style" of the Vita Nuova.".—Professor Giuseppe Mazzotta Sonnets, ballads and *canzone,* or songs—intended to be sung.

xiii **prose & poetry***: vita nova* is written in prosimetrum style, a combination of prose and verse. There are 42 transformations and "situations," Professor Mazzotta calls them, that divide the work and of those there are 31 poems. The verses include the sonnet, ballad and canzone, or song, forms. In almost all the sections, poetry follows the prose on which it is based and is particularized. After the majority of the poems, Dante wafts teacher-like and explains their structure & content; thusly, after the sonnet that begins To every loving heart & captive soul: "This sonnet is divided into two parts. In the first part I _____, while in the second part I _____." Also, he indicated where each part began, i.e.: "The first part begins_____." The reason for this guidance could have been Dante's desire to make his poetry comprehensible to women and men of all classes and education. (also see note p.4 by Professor Aresu.)

xiv Boccaccio marginalizes Dante's commentaries on the poems but keeps the more narrative prose section in the main text. This is the translation (by Jason M. Houston) of Boccaccio's explanation (a quick note that we call 'meraviglierannosi molti' from its incipit):

"A great many will wonder, by what I am claiming, why I have not placed the divisions *(divisioni)* of the sonnets in the text as the author of the present little book placed them; but I reply that there were two reasons for this. First, since the divisions of the sonnets are obviously explanations *(dichiarazione)* of those sonnets, it is apparent that they must be gloss *(chiosa)* rather than text; and thus I set them down as gloss, not text, the one and the other not mixing well together. And were someone perhaps to argue here that both the expositions *(teme)* of the sonnets and *canzoni* written by him could likewise be called glosses in that they are no less explanations of the poems than the divisions are--I maintain that although they are explanations, they are not explanations having the purpose of explaining but demonstrations of the reasons that induced him to write the sonnets and *canzoni*. And it is also apparent that these demonstrations are part of his main purpose; thus deservedly they are text and not gloss. The second reason is that, as I have many times heard said by persons worthy of trust, Dante, having composed this little book in his youth, and having then over time grown in knowledge and in expertise, felt ashamed of having written it, since it seemed very

immature to him. And among the other things he was sorry for having done, he regretted having included the divisions in the text, perhaps for that same reason that moves me; and so, being unable to emend any of the others, in the one I have written I have sought to satisfy the author's wishes".
--Professor F. M. Aresu


An exchange between Anthony Valerio and Professor Aresu—

AV: "I sense that D.'s breakdowns, explanations of each verse were important to him & therefore a crucial part of the tri-partita (prose, verse, explanations of verses.) not gloss. The explanations are easily skipped over but I'd consider whether he wanted them in for the obvious purpose of being clear, not presuming his verse would be easily understood, which often it is not, even pressing clarity to the point of awkwardness."

Prof. Aresu-

"I am in total agreement."


[xv] Famous poets of the time: who also wrote in the vernacular: Dante di Maiano, Cino di Pistoia, Guittone di Arrezo, Guido Calvalcanti. The custom of emerging writers sending their work to established writers continues to this day (2016).


[xvi] Guido Cavalcanti (1255-1300) a fellow Florentine, poet and along with Dante a founding member of the Tuscan poetic style coined by Dante as *dolce stil novo* (see also note p. 35). Cavalcanti strongly

supported Dante writing in the vernacular and in this way was an important behind-the-scenes influence on the creation of the "Italian" language. Dante dedicated his *Vita nuova* to Cavalcanti.

Certainly as was his relationship to his mentor & teacher Bruno Latini, Dante's liaisons with close friends were complicated. Though counting Cavalcanti his best friend, when Dante became one of the priors of Florence he concurred with the decision to exile Cavalcanti, who contracted malaria during the banishment and died in August 1300. Though in the *Inferno* (X) Dante composed a monument to his great friend, I am impressed by the idea that one could banish a best friend to hell for reasons that supersede those of the formation and foundation of the friendship itself—love, respect, loyalty, steadfastness—those alienating reasons being more of a political nature than personal or collegial, like belonging to a oppositional political party, and a stark difference in religious belief: it's said that Cavalcanti was an atheist and fostered, also foisted upon others his non-belief.

[xvii] Dante received, in addition to Cavalcanti's, two other replies: one from the famous poet Cino da Pistoia, the other from Dante de Maiano.

[xviii] *serventese:* poetic form derived from the Provençal poets; originally a poem of service or honor then acquired the character of a poem of praise or satire. Sometimes written in eight-line stanzas, sometimes in quatrains. Commonly in triplets interwoven with the rhyme.

xix "O you who travel"— note regarding this sonnet from the VN's translation by Charles Eliot Norton, ©Houghton Mifflin and Co, 1892: "This poem belongs to the class of what are called *sonnetti doppi*— doubled sonnets...composed of two sextets followed by two quatrains instead of being formed as a regular sonnet of two quatrains followed by two triplets.

xx Love's center of a circle, according to Dante Gabriel Rossetti: "I am the centre of a circle (*Amor che muove il sole e l'altre stelle*): therefore all lovable objects, whether in heaven or earth, or any part of the circle's circumference, are equally near to me. Not so thou, who wilt one day lose Beatrice when she goes to heaven." The phrase would thus contain an intimation of the death of Beatrice, accounting for Dante being next told not to inquire the meaning of the speech,—"Demand no more than may be useful to thee." Also, Buddhists speak of chanting's value as "centering," meaning, perhaps, that internal and external forces are joined, certainly are in balance. Personified Love preaches and admonishes in one breath.

xxi "Don't ask more than's useful to you"—words similar to St. Paul, Romans xii, 3.

xxii ballad: a dance-song beginning with a *ripresa* of three or four line, followed by one or more uniform stanzas, each stanza's last line rhyming with one of the *ripresa's* lines. Like the sonnet and *canzone,* the ballad, set to music, was intended to be sung. Dante wrote the lyrics, one could wonder whether he also composed music and sang

xxiii Wedding ritual. Three years after the passage of their second nine years, Beatrice married Simone de' Bardi, a banker. Mention of this turn of events is nowhere found in their little book, adding, perhaps, to the unexpressed quotient of Dante's grief. Here, each invited guest could bring a companion. Apparently, Dante's friend had been invited and brought him. Dante does not identify this friend. Barbara Reynolds reports that a knight was entitled to bring four companions, judges and doctors three. Dante's friend was not one of these. Some commentators state that the marriage refers to that of Beatrice. Which Charles Eliot Norton rejects: "If the beloved of Dante was, as has been generally supposed, on the untrustworthy authority of Boccaccio, the daughter of Folco Portinari, she was married some time before January 1287, for the will of her father, which is dated on the 15th of that month, contains the following clause: 'Item: to Mistress Bice his daughter, wife of Master Simon de Bardi, he bequeaths fifty florins.' In the spring of 1290, Beatrice died. In 1291, Dante married Gemma dei' Donati... I am disposed...to believe that nothing is known of her [Beatrice] but what Dante tells...how completely his inner life was that of the imagination, that there is no reference in any of his works to the marriage of Beatrice, or to his own, and no mention of his wife or of his children."
Dinner fare at weddings was composed of three

courses not counting fruit and almonds


xxiv "They knew the working of his heart"—his
attempts at camouflaging his love for Beatrice, so
powerful, had been futile, at least in the eyes of
other women, linking their hearts.


xxv the clear Arno—Dante does not name Florence's
main river. The stream of very clear water could also
have been one of the many streams that water
Florence's countryside. We his readers know and do
not know. Often, in VN, Dante does not want his
readers to confine themselves to particulars of
his, i.e., his name, the name of his town and major
river—rather, to confine ourselves to imaginative
particulars of our own


xxvi *"Donne ch'avete intelletto d'amore..."*: each of this
beautiful *canzone's* stanzas resembles a sonnet in
having 14 verses, two quatrains and two tercets.
The phrase *dolce stil novo* is found in the Dante's
Purg. XXIV: Thus he named this form or school of
poetry practiced by a group of poets headed by
himself as well as Guido Cavalcanti, Lapo Gianni
and Cino da Pistoia. The new style's immediate
predecessor was Guido Guinizelli of Bologna
Guido  Guinizelli  (1230-1276),  Italian  poet,
forerunner and mentor of Dante credited with a first
expression of *dolce stil novo* in his poem *Al cor gentil
ripara sempre amore*. It's said that Dante's notion of
love being inseparable from the gentle heart was
introduced into Italian poetry by Guinizelli, whom
Dante alludes to in the second verse as *il saggio*.

Dante was 11 years old when Guinizelli died but was able to encounter him later on in creative work; in *Purgatory*, xxvi. 91-114, Guido asks, "Why in your speech and gaze do you hold me dear?" and Dante replies, "As long as modern usage lasts, your sweet lines will still make dear their very inks."

Dante's close friend and colleague Guido Cavalcanti and his mentor Guido Guinizelli, one ends in hell, the other in purgatory. Dante's sense of friendship and admiration was/is, in addition to complicated, extremely interesting.

xxvii color of pearl: "Evidently the general meaning is that she was pale but not pallid."—K. McKenzie

xxviii death of Folco Portinari—on December 31, 1289; he had six daughters, including Bice, or Beatrice, and five sons, all named in his will.

xxix suffered great pain: an illness from having recently been out in winter weather grieving over Folco.

xxx *ossana in excelsis:* the greeting given to Christ as he entered Jerusalem. *Mark, XI, 10.*

xxxi lady caring for him: believed to be one of Dante's two step-sisters, born of his father's second marriage.

xxxii *la mirabile* Beatrice—she is real and ideal at the

same time, possessing beauty both physical and angelic. Allessandro D'Ancona (1835 – 9 November 1914) notes, "Here is an atmosphere where human beings can breathe and where angels can live also."

xxxiii banner of the Blessed Virgin Mary: Beatrice is now among the souls close to the Virgin .

xxxiv Beatrice Portinari died in the spring 1290. One year before, Dante served with the cavalry in the great battle of Campaldino, on the eleventh of June, when the Florentines defeated the people of Arezzo. In the autumn of the next year, 1290, when for him, by the death of Beatrice, the city as he says "sat solitary," such refuge as he might find from his grief was sought in action and danger: for we learn from the *Commedia* (Inferno, C. xxi.) that he served in the war then waged by Florence upon Pisa, and was present at the surrender of Caprona.

xxxv the number nine: according to Norton--"The mysterious and mystical properties and relations of numbers were in Dante's time a subject of serious study and held to mathematics proper something of the same relationship as alchemy to chemistry."

xxxvi Ptolemy(Tolomeo): Dante knew the astronomer's works through Alfraganus' compendium *Almagest*. the Arabian, Syrian and Christian calendars: Arabian usage had it that the day began at sunset; hence, the first hour of the night of June 8 in Italy, the day Beatrice died, was the first

hour of June 9 in Arabia. The Syrian calendar had it
that the year began with the first two months called
Tixryn (*Tisirin*), corresponding to our October;
hence, June was the ninth month.

xxxvii princes of the land: one commentator writes
that Dante addressed this letter to Italian Cardinals
in 1314 on the election of a successor to Pope
Clement V (Norton). Most commentators agree that
Dante did not address his letter and had no
intention of sending it. That it was an aborted
method of expressing his grief.

xxxviii sorrow's vehicle—Dante's *canzone* in this
section written in the wake of Beatrice's earthly
death occupies their little book's central position. Its
lyrics are preceded by 15 poems and followed by
15.
K. McKenzie points out the interesting juxtaposition
between the prose account versus the poetry: how
the poetics are more 'dramatic' and how, for
example, in the poetry he begins *in medias res,*
proceeds to the end, then backtracks and relates his
hallucinogenic dream until the ladies in attendance
awaken him. Point is, Dante's hand at poetry was
stronger than his prose, facilitated his great talent.
xxxix *carte tavolette*: "The material was probably
boxwood or old fig, possibly parchment, with a
surface smoothed, cleaned, and carefully printed
with bonedust, in the manner described by Cennini."
Elizabeth J. Pellet.

xl Drawing an angel: inspired by Beatrice, Dante's drawing of an angel in turn inspired poet Robert Browning to write the poem "One Word More" for his wife Elizabeth Barrett Browning, which begins: *Dante once prepared to paint an angel: Whom to please? You whisper "Beatrice."* An interesting couplet goes: *Dante, who loved well because he hated, Hated wickedness that hinders loving.*

xli Dante married Gemma Donati about a year after the death of Beatrice. Rossetti conjectures: "Can Gemma then be "the lady of the window," his love for whom Dante so condemns? Such a passing conjecture (when considered together with the interpretation of this passage in Dante's later work, the *Convito*) would of course imply an admission of what I believe to lie at the heart of all true Dantesque commentary; that is, the existence always of the actual events even where the allegorical superstructure has been raised by Dante himself." Interesting to parallel the facts that there are of Dante's life with mirror instances of his inventions, which, at least to my thinking, are all the more interesting.

xlii pilgrims: it is most likely Easter week when Veronica's divinely imprinted veil is displayed in St. Peter's.

xliii his beautiful face: representation of Jesus' face supposedly impressed on the kerchief of Veronica, or "true image" with which she wiped His face on his way to Calvary. It is preserved in St. Peter's.

eyes: D. McKenzie ventures that, for Dante, Love was said to begin in the eyes. As for the mouth, Dante speaks of it as *fine d'amore*, because *lo saluto di questa donna* was for a long time his supreme desire. I have also noted that, in VN, projecting their importance to him, Dante focuses on eyes more than any other facial feature.


xliv The shrine of St. James: in Galicia, a popular resort of pilgrims during The Middle Ages. Santiago: Spain's military patron was one of Christendom's most popular saints.


# Acknowledgements & Sources

Enormous thanks go out to Professor Rebecca West, Professor Giuseppe Mazzotta, Professor Francesco Marco Aresu, Professor Keala J. Jewel and Professor Ellen V. Nerenberg for their invaluable contributions, patience and encouragement.

Of course from Dante Alighieri I had the original text before me. How can artists and scholars thank him enough.

# Bibliography

Digital Dante-Columbia University --
http://digitaldante.columbia.edu/

*The New Life* – Translated with Essays and Notes
by Charles Eliot Norton. Houghton, Mifflin and
Co. (1892).

*La Vita Nova* – translated with an Introduction
by Barbara Reynolds. Revised Edition (2004).
Penguin Books.

*Vita Nuova* – Translated with an Introduction by
Mark Musa. Oxford University Press (1992).

*La Vita Nuova* – Edited with Introduction, Notes,
and Vocabulary by Kenneth McKenzie. D. C
Heath & Co. (1922).

Anthony Valerio is the author of nine books of fiction and non-fiction. His latest publication is IMMIGRANTS according to Anthony Valerio -- Volumes I & II(paperback). He has been a book editor at major publishing houses, including McGraw-Hill and Bantam. His short stories have appeared in the *Paris Review* and his work has been included in readers and anthologized by The Viking Press and Random House. Mr. Valerio has taught at New York University, the City University of New York and Wesleyan University. He is a member of PEN and The Authors Guild.

www.ingramcontent.com/pod-product-compliance
Lightning Source LLC
Chambersburg PA
CBHW030552130626
46552CB00006B/2524